The Main Squeeze

The Main Squeeze

JEFF JOHNSON

Via Dolorosa Press
701 East Schaaf Road, Cleveland, Ohio 44131-1227 USA.
Attn: Hyacinthe L. Raven, ed.

First published 2002 by Via Dolorosa Press

ISBN 0-9718673-0-5

An excerpt from this story appeared earlier in
The Albany Review.

Cover Design: Gene Floersch
Cover Photo: Kathleen Jaeger

Thanks to Mitch, Driver, the Fudds
and Carla.

Joe

Rita's in the bathroom blowing rails. She's got a mirror in her lap, head bent to it. She likes the cool tile. And she likes to comb her hair, really long hair to hide the scar on her neck...

When I cross she looks up.

"Want one?"

I remember Joe, before, staring in the mirror, gun in his mouth. The empty sound it made when he pulled the trigger, like a car door slamming.

She follows me to the kitchen, sits across the table, starts dealing Solitaire. Throws seven cards, then flips a joker.

"For me," she says, "that's a king." I flash on Joe swinging a gun up casually to her chest, rocking back the hammer and firing in one quick move. Just the click, no blast. Rita laughing after her face comes back together.

I pour a cup of coffee. She's dancing by the stereo. When the song gets to the lines she likes, she says them out loud.

"Think of the fun, think of the palm trees."

The singer sounds like his lip's busted.

"Think of the weed, think of the taxis."

Rita doesn't sing, just mouths the words, her head cocked like she's listening to something farther away. I remember her balling Joe last Halloween. I walk through the door and they're on the couch. They freeze and look at me, wearing identical masks, and for a second I can't tell who's who.

But the coffee's too hot, so I let it sit. It's raining and water's blowing through the screen over the sink. Rita comes back and sits down. Another song starts. One I recognize called Snuff It.

"Miss your girlfriend?"

She means Lena. I shrug. I've been hungry for years, hungry for people who aren't around anymore, who seem more alive now they're dead.

"You're better than Eddie at playing possum." She tries to light a cigarette but can't make it because she's laughing, finally drops her arms, takes a deep breath, tries again and gets it, smokes it to the filter.

When I leave, the rain's stopped. I lie in bed and try to think of Lena, not here but in her bed, her spider plants draped from the ceiling in macramé hangers. She'd close her eyes, concentrating on her hit, shoulders back, sheet crumpled in her lap, then she'd blow the smoke slowly toward the window and away from her plants, cupping her hand beneath the ash. "The color of your eyes," she said, leaning toward me for a kiss. But inside her photo album was all I knew would claim her: mother and father in suits, younger brother in a high school jersey, her sorority shot, the family's three-story brick and wood house, the whole scene making me sick but like Lena was none of it there now with me, toking the last few hits, laying open the photo album at her graduation portrait: rouged skin, hair teased right, smile that didn't seem to fit but somehow looked perfect that way...

Once we were at this party. The first thing she said when we got alone was, "You look like you're by yourself too much. You live inside instead of out."

"How do you know," I said, "if I'm alone or bored?"

Lena drained her rum. "Being alone is boring."

A pop song came on I didn't recognize. She stood up and started dancing by herself, moving in her own part of the room, but came back when the song was over.

"Don't you like music?"

I hadn't had anything to do with music for years, but she liked music, the kind that's easy to get into. It fit her.

"Everyone needs friends," she said. "Look at these people. It's a party. Everyone gets loaded, gets some laughs. If you don't come here for that, what do you come for?"

I lit a joint and smoked half and she

came back with a fresh drink and took a few hits. Another song came on she liked - she liked them all - one they play until it sticks in your head even if you hate it. She started dancing by herself, and I watched her until the song was over: weaving around the other dancers, smiling like slipping into a dream that's only rum and grass, and when she came back this time she sat in front of me on the floor, draped her arms over my knees.

"Your color is blue. We all have colors, and yours is blue. It's for people like you, who live inside."

"What's yours?" I asked, and suddenly Eddie turned up beside me. I wondered where he'd been, where he'd gone to blast up. I wondered what his color was.

"Yellow," Lena said. "The color of the sun, vitality."

But this chick was all over Eddie, blasting coke off a piece of mirror, going on about how she "can't get no strange," makes it alone now. I watched her rip a line, sit back and hold her face at an angle to keep her nose packed.

"Fucking hot party," she said. But Eddie wasn't even dressed. He didn't even look at her. He just handed over his Heineken.

Later, Lena stretched out beside me, fastened her hair out of the way and painted this bird trailing long flames on my back, the wings soft acrylic cuts. At Joe's, I stood on the edge of the tub, twisted around to look at it over my shoulder in the mirror, the gold and blue-tipped fire tearing away from its breast and neck and wings burning through the soap film. Then Rita walked in.

"Clean," she said

It wore off in a week.

Lena

I try to catch a sound to hang on to: a spider picking its way across the floor, the steady scream of a cricket, the waves down on the beach. But all I get is the faint hum of the fan. So I slip back to this night Lena and I went looking for turtles, hoping to catch one dragging itself out of the surf to lay eggs along the dune line. She brought a flashlight but wouldn't turn it on, saying the light would scare them. I told her once they get started they can't stop. We walked about three miles before she thought she saw one, but it was only a stump of driftwood wedged in jeep ruts. Then we found tracks where one had been maybe a few hours before.

"Look at the angle," she said. "How they come out and go back in like a wishbone, like a woman's legs, and here, where the eggs are buried."

But up the beach was music in the wind. We followed it to the seawall. A band for servicemen at the NCO Club. Lena said something I couldn't hear, but I nodded like I understood and kept watching the band and the dancers, the men's shirts sticking to their backs from the sweat, the women in tight dresses and heels.

That night I was on her couch scraping the roaches out of the ashtray and tearing off the paper to roll a pinner when she came in out of the bedroom yelling, "Say it, just say you don't like fucking me." Then she started crying so I held her for a while. When she got straight she opened a bottle of wine but didn't pour it, just started digging through her pencil box.

"All the colors in Crayola Crayons and they still invent new ones."

"What color?" I asked, but she didn't say anything, so I hit the wine and started spinning her hanging plants.

"You can't sleep here," she said, not looking up from her drawing, all that charcoal hair in her face. I ran my hand along the curve of her back, caught the patchouli that smelled like her sheets. She stood up and walked back to the bedroom without saying a word. I thought about kicking in the door, but instead I searched the fridge for a beer, found some rum under the sink, sat on the couch drinking, a plant dripping on my shoulder. Ten minutes later she came back out, knelt at my feet with her head in my lap and asked me what I'd do if I had money. I said it depended on how much. She said a few thousand. I said I'd buy a car, a convertible, then I'd drive it somewhere.

She said, "I'll write you a check."

Then she dragged the sheet to the chair where she'd thrown her jeans, found her checkbook.

"How much?"

"You wouldn't."

"Pretend I did," she said. "You'd take it, wouldn't you?"

I get up and cross the hall. The light's on in the kitchen but no one's there. When I lie back down again the light jumps from the candle to the wall, like something's going to happen, but nothing happens. A spider as big as my fist is straight above and behind me on the wall, and I think how just before Eddie split he told me spiders were in his dreams. I pick up the candle and raise it over my head. I hear the sound of rain, so I know I've been sleeping, but not for long, though it's already dark out from the storm. I don't see the spider, then I feel it on my cheek, jump up slapping at my face, my hair, kneel on the floor shaking out the sheets to find it, brush it off my leg, look for something to kill it with, but it's back on the wall in the corner like it never moved. I lie down sweating, heartbeat like good meth, squeeze my eyes but it's still right there...

Library lights are on. I push open the glass door that says pull. So quiet inside I'd like to scream at everyone to shut up. Flip them. Shut the fuck, really loud. But I want this place like a good bar where no one hassles you, no one even looks up when you walk in. I find a mag on the rack and sit back into a soft vinyl chair, the hum of the air-con all over me. I thumb through the pictures but can't concentrate. There's this old man across from me, sleeping. Sleeping in the goddamn library. Practicing death, and no long wait. Not that he's making any noise, not snoring or anything, just sleeping there, right out in the middle of the place, in a chair pulled out from one of the tables by the rack of junk records and encyclopedias, then he's getting up, the strain in his face like he's climbing off a toilet, not dead, maybe not even sleeping, maybe thinking, maybe waiting for this mag I'm reading, waiting to read the jokes. I read the jokes, and none are as funny as this old man changing chairs from one facing north to one facing west: there's no difference, and the light's the same. But he goes right back into it: chin down, hands folded over his guts.

I feel an urge to wake him up. Get his nerve back. But I can't do anything with him staring at me out of his sleep. I walk over and stand right in front of him, throw the mag down on the table. He doesn't move, so I leave him and the magazine and walk to the bathroom. It's locked, the sign says, "Due to vandalism." The librarian at the desk has the key. She's around thirty-five (I guess), and her hair's cut perfectly to shape her face. She ignores me at first, then looks me over, gets it all in an instant. She doesn't dig me but she's not disgusted. She might be a mother, but I hope not. She hands over the key and I open the door. Inside's so clean it stinks. The walls are poisoned with disinfectant. I step into a stall, shut the door and lock it, drop the seat and sit down. The key's attached to a large square piece of hard plastic with LIBRARY stamped on it. The surface is smooth, though, so I pull out the little plastic bag Joe gave me and use the key to cut open the top of the bag. I lay the key ring across my knees and pour out a pile, but I don't have anything to blast with. Even if I'd asked the desk clerk for a Bic she'd think I was writing on the walls. I think of looking calmly up at her and explaining, no, what I'll do is jerk the insides out and use the shell to whiff up a quarter G. So I stare at the powder, each flake edge scintillating in the hard light of the bathroom, and think of what I might do: take a pile out to the old man and hold it under his nose, nudge him enough to get him one good blast. Instead I lift the block off my knees and snort hard, brush the flakes off my face, careful to keep them falling back on the plastic, then lift it again for another hit. This time the coke bites. I get the drip. Scrape up a small pile, wait, for the feeling. But nothing happens. I do what's left. My throat goes numb. I lick the bag, the key chain. My nose is bleeding. Still, nothing.

I drop the key chain on the counter. The lady's in the back bent over a table. I hesitate, watching her, tracing the belt of flesh where her sweater rides up over her slacks, and I feel like showing her the plastic on the key chain all smeared with saliva and tiny crystals melting like snowflakes. Had she seen snow? On a hot window? I'd seen snow once, in North Carolina. I followed Lena there, found her cottage, dropped by like she'd still be open to me, but the hour I showed up the snow began and we watched it, the three of us, me for the first time, millions of flakes falling out of the blackness into the light of the room dying on the window. We drank warm brandy while Lena explained what a good year it had been for whatever it was her husband was doing for a living, watching how the light caught the side of her face, believing she'd come to me like before while her husband slept or died, but the evening went on quietly until the streaks of melting snow turned to rain, and I could only remember how she looked in her kitchen, her thin fingers gathering mushrooms and slicing the caps on the terra cotta plates her mother had given her, when I was the one she was cooking for.

I make it outside and smell the trees, but when I hit the yellow in the first store window I think I'm going to be sick. I remember how the other night when Joe laid the bag on me, Rita came out of the bathroom from taking a shower wearing only a towel, her hair combed straight and drawn back from her forehead, her eyes free of makeup. She stopped me in the hallway, right beside Joe in his room, unfurled the towel, watching me, smiling, her hair almost blue in the hall light.

Inside a restaurant the tables are spread out on a sand-colored tile floor. Plate-glass front and sides. Fake wood paneling. Red vinyl-covered stools along the counter, same red vinyl seats in the booths along the wall. No one looks up. The waitress yells into the kitchen: "Make it rare." Then she glances at me. I sit in front of the big polished coffee urn. She comes over, a slim brunette whose eyes look beaten up. I order coffee black.

But there's a girl in the corner wearing a dark blouse and jeans. She's got mauve sunglasses that glow almost neon against her olive skin. I get the feeling I know her, that at least I'd met her before or seen her somewhere, but I look away to the mirror behind the stack of glasses and coffee packs and the pastel porcelain juice squeezer and milk shake machine. I stay in the mirror to keep from watching the girl, but the whole time I feel like she's watching me, and that's when I see another guy in the corner I'd missed, his shoulders and elbows torn through his shirt, cloth like strands of nerves. I catch his shoes, new ones with thick rubber soles and suede the earthniks sell down at the Co-op. He's eating steak and eggs, pushing the stuff around his plate with a piece of toast. I try not to watch, but in the whole place there's nothing I can't see. I stand by the stool and stuff in my shirt, see the bathroom and go for it, flip on the dull yellow inside with the door shut and wash my face, avoiding the mirror until I look up, relieved, seeing there's not one in the frame.

Outside, the coffee kicks in on the cocaine. There's a Laundromat next door. I'm watching the dryers spin when I see the chick with the electric shades cross the street for a bar two blocks over, so I follow her. But when she slides in past the doorman, I hang out on the porch. The deck goes toward the beach on pilings. The wood's rotten and the porch sags to the south. There's no wind, no waves, totally calm between the storms, the gray deck glistening from the earlier rain. I find a half-empty glass of beer, warm but not flat.

When I see her she isn't wearing the

glasses. She's with two other girls. I'm leaning in the doorway beside the jukebox and the music's making me sick, but I look obvious until one of her friends squeezes by me through the doorway.

"Want one?"

I nod as she passes and go over to the girl.

"Out for a drink?"

"Just out."

"All three?"

"We came in the same car."

"You driving?"

The other girl comes back with the beer. I take mine.

"You have a car?"

"I didn't say that."

I let it go and drink without saying anything. She's talking to her friends so I sit back and scan the bar and finish the beer, but I'm aching for this chick. For when I get her alone. For what she thinks she needs. I start to leave and she asks me what I'm doing.

"Let's split," I say. "Smoke a joint." I know she's in now and I'm trying to cut it short, but it's still too fast and she's hanging back.

"Walk?"

"Down the beach."

Now she has a reason to lay on the others. I should've said whiff. Coke would've been a smarter lie. She says something to the others I can't hear, but when she sits up she says let's go.

On the beach I feel a fresh rush from the coke, then I get where I am and it seems like I've been following her across the sand for hours. Once out of the lights I stop and pull her to me. She kisses with her tongue and slips her hands under my shirt, but I break it off and swing up toward the bank leading to the street. She holds back, asking about the joint, follows anyway, complains a little but I don't catch what she's saying, and when we get to the steps we try the routine. But she keeps mashing away at me, laughing. "Are you drunk already?"

I try to back off. "Listen," I say, and we almost fall off the steps. "Wait." Then I shove her down and everything goes real slow. I see her face in the sand and her hands out by the sides of her head like she's feeling for her glasses.

"Goddamn you," she says, brushing sand off her face. "Goddamn you motherfucker."

She keeps saying it over and over. I reach for her, to help her up, but instead run across the paved lot at the top, stop by a transformer box and kneel to catch my breath, the coke edge going dull from the beer, then run some more along the road

until I go back down a few blocks south, strip
in a clump of sawgrass. The water's cold from
the rain, and the moon's shiny like tin foil. I
dive under, lie face down on the bottom, feel
each wave pass, pull back, then in again with
the next swell, and there's Lena, clear as ever.
And this time, as I walk her from the bar, I
hold her head between my hands and take her
under, wash the sand out of her hair, rinse her
eyes, and she's not breathing but lying still
with me watching the stars burn below us.
Then dragging a long way out along the
bottom, she's gone.

Rita

Joe's on his way to the matinee at this topless bar downtown. First thing he notices is my hand's stitched up, still fresh, so I tell him about the nail gun and the nail in my hand, how when you see a nail in your hand you know how wrong it is...

He's driving an El Dorado convertible. The panels are rusted out. The ragtop's shaky. The rings are shot. Oil smokes off the block. But the radio's loud. He's talking about a girl he "got into movies," another he kept locked up in his room for a week. He tells about a girl he "sees" who can't speak English, and one he says pays for visits.

But when he starts about Rita, I pass the rum and don't say anything, because with Rita, the longer you stay, the harder it is to go back.

"Yeah, and with her," he says, "never let her know what you like."

I drink his rum, dig the breeze, pick at my stitches, remember Rita hiking her skirt to her waist, taking a shot in her crotch, getting off fast, confessing that first night I met her how she could never get straight enough to operate anything, and that when she waitressed she kept dropping trays. But she got shots free, and never mentioned money ... later, cooling down with vodka, it was one of those cases where you drop by for a minute and stay a month. Because what she hated was shooting herself. And that's what I was for ... it didn't matter what she was shooting. It was my shooting her, looking for a clean spot to hit. It was like, everywhere I touched I left a bruise...

But now inside Rita's grinding on a raised cement dance floor, practiced in heels, some guy slipping bills in her G-string, dancing stuff she should've forgotten...

"Say you're glad to see me," she says, blowing smoke up into the bar lights, her face changing color with the Budweiser sign. "Tell me I look great. Tell me you see a difference."

I don't tell her anything. She leans in close, says, "Well I changed. I'm clean."

Even in the dull neon I can see her scar, her smile too straight. But she's not clean.

"Sure," I tell her.

Then Joe cuts in - "Clean is not the word." - hands her a rum and coke. She ignores the drink, stares at her cigarette. He tells a joke and leaves. What's he regret? Where else could he be? Joe, who knows all the excuses. Who talks even when people don't listen. But I listen. And he talks darts and cars and pool and women. Flashing a red bandana, cowboy boots. That's what I like:

consistency. Boots and jeans, rum and coke, stories too sick to be lies...

Once Rita rented this place on the beach so expensive we left the furniture covered, slept nights on the porch. Worked off her shots with an AM transistor, surgically dialing endless channels, the sessions like all-day radio shows broken up by storms off the ocean. The rain in sheets at the edge of the beach kept us wet all night, Rita combing her hair, tuning the radio. And once between the crack in the music and the ozone burning before the rain she told me how you measure distance by thunder, but when the lightning hit outside she started reciting dreams: being held underwater, surviving airline crashes, leading strangers through tunnels, a day book of miracles. Monday, one about flying. Tuesday, animals. Wednesday - but by then she was in the yard, in the sea oats, lightning strobing around her ...

Joe wins at darts, buys the drinks.

"You need an eye," he says. "Instinct."

Throws again: zero.

"Either way," he says, and hands me a dart. "You don't trust yourself, you lose."

I run my thumb along the feathers, push the shaft through my fingers like a plunger, think of the eye Joe needs for darts, the blind tip sailing home.

"It's in the wrist," he says. "The

touch."

The tip's dull but draws blood. I pick at my stitches and think tetanus ... finally get Rita in a corner by the DJ's booth and order a lap dance for a chance to talk. I slip dollar bills in her garter while she grinds. She's gained weight. She looks soft. Not so yellow. But when she asks about my hand, I shove her over.

"I changed," she says. "I got Jesus."

I pop a buck in her garter. "Same junkie to me."

Outside the sun's almost gone but the heat's like a hammer. I put the top up on the El Dorado, crawl in the back seat, not the sky in the post cards, no cottage view of the beach. No night storms, no sea breeze. I'm downtown. It's a topless bar. A concrete block hut. A few pickup trucks. A Camaro.

I find a Phillips head in the floor of the car, dig out a stitch. I see Joe of the "good eye," of "instinct," making it, but what he doesn't know is Rita with a needle between us. Rita, in October, in a wet summer dress, finally coming out with how she measured our sex, in grams, in frequency. Nights with the radio, trying to get out of her dress. "But you have to," she says, so I nick her with the needle, her shoulders, back of her neck, while she's trying to find a channel from another night, thumbing the tuner, more frantic every minute with the dial.

She said the shots are simple, a thing you don't mix up, even if you dream at night, of the strip routine, another wet dress, the soft resistance of her skin.

Inside I hit a booth in the back so I can't see the stage. But I can hear the music. I know she's dancing in some spangled G-string, a dip in her grind. Joe's at the pool table with his friends, but nobody's shooting. Place smells like carpet cleaner and something frying in the kitchen. Then I remember: people live here. The guy behind the bar, his wife and kids: barefoot pre-teens, taking turns coming up front for the guy to send White Russians back to the old lady. I wonder if they dance, if they like the music, and start to follow but Joe's in the booth, sleeves rolled to his tattoos.

"Wait'll they put those babes to work," he says, coming back to Rita. "Around other people," he says, "concentrate on what you see, not what they're watching. That way you don't think much, you know, to keep up."

I think of Rita, concentrating ... not now, not in this music, that grinding she's tithing to Jesus, but back then, on a curve of beach, in lightning ... she wasn't thinking. She was talking on top of the radio about sharks and sand dunes, the strike of each channel, of patterns in shells, crowding the couch up against a window ...

Joe's not forgetting either: "These are friends, right? But what is 'friend'? That shit gets to you, man. You gotta have somebody to fuck with, somebody to fuck with you. It's normal."

The jukebox cuts into the bar sound system. There's a skip, then everybody's covered, and Joe holds his cue stick like a guitar.

So I tell him, I can't see it with Rita.

"Just a party," he says, and throws a can.

She wraps her robe around her sandals. Her eye shadow's got glitter in it. She looks cheap, but somehow right that way. And then I miss her for the robe, those fake Palm Beach sandals, dream how she comes to the shots again, to that beach house, the radio nights on the porch.

I tell her, he wants a party.

She says, "He's in the right place."

"After," I tell her.

"After," she says, "I go home."

She looks like she needs a cigarette. Nervous. From me? From what she remembers? Or from wracking up her spirit in that

Christian scheme of things?

"I'll call the cops."

"For a party?"

"They'll send a car," she says. And believes it. So I tell Joe she's changed.

"You don't change," he says. "From that."

"She's a freak," I tell him. "All prayers and tears." Catch myself taking Joe seriously: eyeballing a fake shot, cue stick behind his back. His friends watch like it's real. "Even better," he says. "Even better, because that way, we can give her back what's missing."

I catch the end of Rita's show. She's in the G-string and heels, wallowing in some guy's lap must be sixty.

"She's clean," I tell him.

"Forget it," he says, like he's shooting again. "We'll keep it friendly."

Rita calls her trailer a "mobile home," but there's nothing mobile about it. Parked up on cement blocks, corrugated porch roof sagging off the back. Inside, all direct lighting and eighth-inch paneling. Floor cushions everywhere.

She's dusting herself with baby powder, glad I'm there, hoped all those months, she says, I'd stop by. I'm looking at this pamphlet she's got out, asks me am I going to heaven. Places all over the world send you stuff, on how to get in, even me, like a club that takes anybody who can pass initiation. And there's a test that asks you questions, only none of the choices are right, and none are what you can think up on your own. Then they list some other words, and you pick the ones that best describe God, but none are wrong. You can't lose. Then they say, even then, with all those solid words for God, He's even greater than what the list pretends.

But Rita's in a teddy and a see-through robe, stands over me when I lean back out of the light. Lap dance? She turns the page.

"See here how in the left column it says men can be kind or loving or good, and how over in the right-hand column it says destructive or selfish or - "

I take the column on the left.

"You lie," she says.

"It's easier," I tell her, waiting for a dance. She says I miss the point. "In love," she says, "Jesus lives."

I slip a dollar in her teddy.

"He died for you," she says.

I tell her He asked for it.

"On a cross," she says. "Nobody deserves that."

I throw another dollar and she backs off.

"You gotta feel Jesus," she says, "inside

you." But I'm listening for the rain, slow at first, then the trailer's roaring in a downpour. I pull the curtain back to the jalousie glass. Rita's got a candle going, smells like peppermint, and just as quick the rain quits, the trailer fills with smoke. And that's when she starts dancing. Just throws open her robe, singing to herself, going into it. Chanting: "Open your heart. Accept right motives. Love Jesus" - on obedience to God and service to others when I tell her I want her on needles.

She goes into how she's "into" life, how she's "thinking positive," how she's "evolved."

On her knees now.

"Jesus is love," she says. "Jesus is truth. I got it in me."

I put the candle out, bend her over my lap, kiss her scars, the ones I'd given her, the one she gave herself. She's going on about the good side of people, trying to get at my face. I got her robe pushed off her shoulders, read the fading scars like a relief map of our time together.

But when she rolls off, I hold her still, listen for Joe, lean down close with the screwdriver by her ear.

"All that time," she says, "It wasn't the shots." I draw a line across her back with the Phillips head. "I haven't had a shot since Christmas."

Anything can happen, but I just open the trailer door. It's raining. My hand's bleeding. It's a long walk back to the bar, but the rain cools me off, and when I'm there the door's a breeze, not even a dead bolt. Inside looks smaller, darker, like a rec room in a split-level more than a tit joint. I cut on the Budweiser sign, and all the other neon. Cut the lights on over the pool tables, the ones behind the bar, in the plastic red shades along the back wall, and except for the people, the noise, the buzz, the place looks right again.

So I go in the bathroom, just renovated: new toilet, new fake wood paneling, new black-caulked tile. Paint still smells poison. Above the sink where the mirror should be, somebody's carved "Fuck me" and a number.

I go to their room first. Big bed in a corner, TV and sofa out in the middle, some furniture from the dressing rooms downstairs pushed against the wall. The wife snores. Up close, I can smell the White Russians on her breath. Her husband's comatose on ludes or Demerol or codeine - a basket of scripts on the dresser. His wife's eyes flutter. With the tip of the screwdriver, I push her cheek into a smile.

The girls' room is different. About the size of a big closet, the ceiling slanting to a dormer window so you have to stoop by the bed. The girls sleep together. I lie on the floor, listen to their breathing, to the rain, to the rattle of the AC wall unit in the other room, remember Rita saying how easy it is to end up like this: a script for Demerol, a wife on vodka, mortgaged up the ass with a couple kids. But I just lie there, and when the rain stops, the wall unit stops too, and I think somebody's up. The floor creaks. One of the girls says something and rolls over. Then the wall unit kicks in again. I get up, close. Their toenails and fingernails are painted red, they smell like chocolate and their feet are dirty, and I can hear, that close, the sounds they make in their dreams...

It's dawn by the time I watch from the hall: he's choking her, on his knees, behind her, shouting. She's thrashing in the sheets.

Downstairs the sound's worse, louder. The lights are still on. The beer lights. The bar lights. Pool lights. Booths. Not as sharp with the sun up, but enough for the difference between the room, now, and what's upstairs. So I feed the jukebox, hit some numbers: make the guy choose...

The clouds burn off in the sun. Steam hangs in the street. By the time I get to Rita I'm wet again, but just push in, like Joe never made it, and the room looks good: nothing's broken. Only small noises: a wind-up clock, a circulating fan, a drip in the sink, the sound Rita's making, that she lives by, in the other room.

She's not bad. Just backed against the wall, talking to herself.

"Rita," I say. "Rita, shut up."

But she keeps it up, her eyes smeared, robe ripped off her shoulder. Bible stuff, prayers, verse, like a radio preacher. I find the red bandana, a towel to wrap her in. She grabs a plastic crucifix off the wall. "Love Jesus," she says. "You got to love Jesus."

I find some matches, get a candle going on the nightstand. Even in the daylight coming through the jalousie the light throws shadows in the room, the scent still strong from last night. I put my face in her hair - smells like mildew and peppermint, sweat and rum and smoke - tie it back with the bandana, ease her into bed. She slips off her broken heels, the spike still hinged to one shoe. I get the bath going, one of those plastic tubs that creaks when you're in it, but the pressure's good, so I let it run till it's steaming, and she's naked now, the crucifix in one hand, broken shoe in the other: I rip the heel off and she takes it like a crayon, like she's gonna draw on the walls, the sheet. The sound of the bath fills the room, the fan useless in the heat. "I'm moving back," she tells me, "to the beach." Kisses her crucifix - another blue-eyed Jesus - sits in the tub while I wash her hair, the crucifix like a doll between her knees, until my stitches come loose and my hand starts bleeding and she tells me what a simple thing it is to pray.

Eddie

The solo white in a black speakeasy: Eddie in his tight sequin dress, wig, heels, about six-two but not clumsy, drinking seven-and-sevens and going off about his boyfriend in county jail, how he was (of course) set up, and how when he gets out he's fixing some guy's ass, and how (of course) when he gets out he's getting Eddie off the street and setting him up housekeeping in this condo they've already picked out - clean now, she says, been clean for two months, and would stay that way when he's out, account of some job somebody's holding him ...

I send her a drink. She takes it without looking up, sweating now, her make-up smeared, the faint shadow of a beard showing through.

"I know you," she tells the bartender. He moves away. "I know what you want," she says.

I try to see the man behind her eyes, all pancake and rouge, tall in her wig and heels - send another seven-and-seven: she's on her last trick when the bartender brings her drink. "We're close," she says, "you and me." He doesn't look at her. Nobody looks. Nobody listens. Just me. I believe her. That her boyfriend's straight, that he's getting out, that he's got a job lined up, that he'll get her off the street.

But this time I send her a gin and tonic. She hesitates when the guy brings it, like seeing a clear drink for the first time. But she belts it and starts about this guy she picked up at the marina turns out to be a "fruit."

Next it's vodka and milk, and she hesitates longer, doesn't even touch the glass. Another rum and coke comes like some health clinic appointment card, some coded reminder.

When she finally looks, finally sees me, I'm sending a tequila, no salt, draft chaser. She's taller than I thought.

"Thanks for the drinks," she says. "But I'm off, okay?"

She tries keeping her accent neutral, but still sounds local. She needs a shave, her wig's too small ... wears her dress like a pro. But her eyes, too soft for how red.

So I tell her I dig her heels.

"Well, baby, these heels," she says, "are no special order. They fit right off the rack."

Then she's going through her shoulder bag - her "apartment" - sets a pair of red patent leather pumps on the bar. "I had to have them. See? These little plastic beads."

I spend the next day, all day, at the post office. Ask the guy five, six times, almost every hour, is there a letter. General delivery. He just walks back somewhere without saying anything, comes up front again and says, "Nothing yet." Believing me. Optimistic. Like a letter was coming. From Lena. Until I tell him maybe he missed it, and he nods at some lady behind me. All I'm saying, I tell him, is you might have missed it.

"Next," he says. "Yes, next."

I talked to her, I tell him. Twice.

The lady's not moving. Still, the guy won't look at me.

It's not just a letter, I tell him. It's an invitation. I show him the bus tickets. Phone numbers I can still use. What do you want, I say, two IDs? I tell him I know where he lives. Where his wife works, where his daughter's in school.

The lady in line starts to leave. I grab her arm. She drops her package. The postal guy looks like he's gonna yell but doesn't. I tell her, "I need that letter."

"There's no letter," the guy says.

"No letter," says the lady. "Believe him."

"There's no letter," the guy says. "I swear."

I pick up the lady's package and hand it to her, tell her how many rides it took to get here. How many drivers I had. What dependency leads to, in the long run.

"What do you think?" I ask the guy. "I'm the one drinking seven-and-sevens? Bragging on my boyfriend, doing three to five for assault?"

"You got no address," the guy says. "What do you expect?"

When I show up on Craven St., Eddie's not there, and this time when the phone rings inside I grab it, can't hear anything for the noise, hang up, drink her seven-and-sevens myself, and by the time she gets there the place is thin. She says it's not her fault, doing what she's doing.

I buy her a drink, finish mine, feel like breaking something, put the glass down carefully, center of the napkin.

We catch a restaurant along Market still serving off the bar menu. She orders oysters Rockefeller, escargot, bottle of wine. Hands me a credit card.

I ask about the boyfriend, what he's in for.

"What everybody's in for," she says. "Being bad."

She eats with her fingers, shows all her teeth when she smiles.

"What about you?" she says. "People

don't just show up this time of year to celebrate the Recovery."

I tell her about brandy in canisters, fires in the living room, every detail, right down to the snow.

"Revenge," she says. "How romantic. You must be in love. But listen, baby" - she dips her fingers in her water glass - "This is no time to hesitate."

We rent a room. I take the floor. She's on the couch. There's no bathroom or shower, so we use her key to the marina. I meet her when she's finished in the club off Craven. By then she's tired of her heels, orders her first seven-and-seven.

Only once I come back to the room and she's still getting dressed, sprawled on her side, up on her elbow, doing her eyes. I get down on the floor with her, start flicking the switch on the light cord.

She goes: "That really bothers me."

And I tell her, don't make it so easy.

But she just keeps doing her eyes. So I cut the light and some blue comes in, not sharp like a cop, but soft, like from a car in fog coming through the window at us. And when she puts her head in my lap, says, "I could love you," I don't move.

She says, "You know how to love me."

And I tell her, yeah, maybe with a knife.

So she comes up with this paring knife - handle cracked, blade rusted loose - tells me how she stole it - starts cleaning it, trying to sharpen it on the edge of the table.

"I'm desperate," she says. "Things are tough. What can I say?"

She's got too much white on, her eyes black with liner.

"But, baby," she says, "this is for you." And she rips out a page of newspaper, wraps the blade, creasing the edges into a tight, neat package.

We're taking the night off, she says, but when she goes out for the stuff I stay in the room. It already smells like I live here, and that's reason enough for leaving, even with the package on the table where she left it. "A birthday present," she says, "whenever your birthday is."

She comes back with corn chips, salsa, jar of olives, a candle she lights and waxes to the table - cuts the lights, she says, like a shrine - "Right, baby? Year of recovery?" - opens everything, arranges it all around the package and the candle, then digs out the gin and vermouth and paper cups. "Wish we had ice," she says. "I really dig these olives."

Her food. Her party. Her night off. She picks at the stuff like she's looking through trash for a phone number.

"You should eat," she says. "But I know you: first sign of weakness, of giving in ... I know what you're thinking, with that girl, that revenge ... I know."

What I know is what keeps her familiar. What'll never change. But she says, "I'm there, baby, and it's not true. You can't give that up, can't afford to. You do that, it's over."

She blows out the candle, touches me again. I feel like breaking her fingers. Until she rubs her face in my hand, finds my scar.

"Nice one," she says, and digs up her flashlight. "Beautiful, the way it healed."

I tell her about the nail gun, how they had to cut it out, how since it started healing I'm losing feeling.

"Good for you, baby," she says. "Good for you."

She's bent close, her flashlight trained on the scar, tracing it with her finger. "Notice how it runs along your lifeline," she says. "You did this for that girl, didn't you? What is she? What're you gonna tell her? What can you do for her? What sort of life?"

I grab her face, hold her tight until the flashlight goes out. In the dark I can't tell if she's listening. She's not sure, I tell her. Of what she gives up.

So when I let her go, she says, "Don't get me wrong, baby. It's his third trip. What's he gonna do?"

She's got the flashlight again, looking for her heels. "What you are is what you lose. In that, we're all the same."

At the bus station, it feels good to watch a bus pull out north every hour. I get the schedule board memorized - the locals, the expresses - they're never on time. The 7:26. The 10:10. The 12:01. Their announced precision a hopeless joke, but reassuring, for the people buying tickets, relieved no matter when the bus gets there by the same promise of arrival, the same need to go.

I meet her later on Craven St. outside the bar going through her bag. Her "apartment." She says she can't find the package. That it's not on her, and it's not in the room.

"And obviously," she says, "you don't have it." She's got all this stuff out on the sidewalk, her mirror, shoes, scarves and junk. "Baby," she says, "you know it was special, between us, you and me."

I order her a seven-and-seven. By the time her drink's melted, I get an early start on my last look around.

Rita

I got the top down, static on the radio. She's huddled by the vent with her bag in the floor, and all I can see is hair, pounds of it, black, bleached in streaks. I punch the El Dorado to get the heater cooking, only by the sound of the engine I don't think it's making it, so I keep it flat out till I'm knocking eighty and she warms up, sits back and asks me why the top's down.

I tell her. She plays with the power windows anyway, the seat switch, spins the radio dial (it's dead too), but when she hits the button for the top and blows the dash lights, I shove her back in her seat, hold her there like she's jumping out. She just knots her hair around her neck and stares down the lights of the cars we're passing.

I hit the first diner we come to, pull right up front, right up into the sterile white lights, right up into the plate glass and steel, and that's when she asks about the pamphlets.

It's a market, I tell her, up north. For a new red-letter healing edition Bible.

Then the dash lights come on, the radio cracks. She squares around in her seat. "We gonna be lovers?"

I tell her to read the pamphlet.

"I had religion," she says. "Now I got options."

She's talking champagne sunsets and ocean terraces, so I just punch it like it never happened. Like we never stopped.

But back on the road she wants food. I string out a line of diners she won't commit to. I keep slowing down so she can check one out, but it's always, "not this one" or "no, not here" and "next one, next one."

When I finally pull over, she's asleep. It's a cinder block and plywood shack with a red and blue sign in the window, gravel parking lot. I leave her wrapped up down in the seat with a towel, the motor running, the heater pathetic. The sky's pocked with stars. There's smoke in the trees. Inside, even above the TV and the jukebox I can hear the El Dorado idling in the lot. They all look, even the kid in the back shooting pool. I get a bottled beer to keep some glass in my hand, finish the first one fast and order another. After all, maybe she'll take the car.

But this kid's watching me more than his shots. I'm thinking: I drove this far to find some country punk in a red shirt flared at the collar - dig out my change - figure, between Rita and this kid, between that sick El Dorado and a game of straight pool, the timing's right. So I try the phone, and when the ringing stops I say, very slow, very clear, deliberate, "Twelve hours." And on the other end, Lena says, "No."

"Twelve hours," I tell her. "Two days, max."

Then Rita comes in, starts shooting with the kid at the back table. A guy at the bar says he'll spot him a beer. So I get a new bottle, but they're watching Rita, and I watch her too - barefoot, shirt open to her waist, tight black spandex top. Got her hair back but it's still long enough to fall when she stretches out of her jeans for a shot. And I think: you get her out of her clothes, there's nothing to see in to, nothing to stretch out of, no faking what she's after - leaning across the table, tossing her hair, taking too long to line up her shot, missing.

"Hey, sport," - the guy at the bar - "Sport, have another beer."

They're playing cut-throat. She's making their night. Still ... he's got a bad limp.

"Or a drink," he says. "But you got to go further up the road, you want a real drink. Here, it's just wine or beer."

If I get off first, there're two other guys, and the bartender, only this new guy starts in on where we're from, where we're going, like we're together, Rita and me, and she's playing along like we're in some honeymoon, only there's no champagne, no sunset, no terrace over the river. Just this kid chalking his stick, this guy with the limp. Across the bar, somebody hangs on the phone, impatient. She says, “I don’t want a drink.” Says, “I want a beer.”

“We play for beers,” the kid says.

“Sure,” I tell him. “Shoot for me.”

The kid screws chalk on his stick. Rita says, “Two hundred and sixteen stitches in my neck” and pulls her hair back to her long blue scar.

“God’s will,” she says, and starts twisting her hair, looking at me like I got her head in my hands, wind coming in the way it does over sixty, some honeymoon opening like stars in the El Dorado...

“Next thing,” she says, “the straight life was fucking me up.”

The kid believes her. He’s smiling and nodding and says, “You bet.”

And then Rita asks him where’s the bathroom. Only she says. “Ladies’ room,” kicks the chair and slams the three ball in the corner.

“Back’re,” the kid says, and she goes, “Show me.”

“God’s will,” he says. The TV comes up. The guy with the limp drills three straight and scratches, goes: “You’re both lying,”

Rita laughs, says: “I wanna drink. You wanna drink?”

But even the kid’s into it: “Where’re

you people from? What're you doing here, middle of nowhere?"

"I'm selling Bibles," I tell the guy. "Pocket-size, red-letter healing edition."

"Bibles," he says. "What you want with Bibles?"

"It's authorized," I tell him. "King James."

The guy racks another game. "I was at revival once," he says. "My mother made me go, for my leg." He makes a tight rack, then shows me how his leg's healed. "Maybe it helped. I don't know. Back then I couldn't even bend my knee."

The kid looks like he's just remembered something funny. "And him and her drinking," he says. "Bible salesman in a place like this."

"These people in here can't even read," the guy says "How can you save yourself if you can't read?"

"Yeah, answer that," the kid says. "Where you gonna send a blind man grows up in a joint like this?"

There's another long moment, but I can hear the El Dorado, steady. Rita smoothes the pamphlet open on the table.

"But you can read," she says. "Read that."

The guy goes for it but the kid gets it. "What?"

"It's a map," she says. "A short cut." Then she laughs off by herself, leaving the kid serious.

"Listen," I tell him. "These Bibles got divine healing commentary, harmony of the Gospels, indexed Bible doctrine, parables and miracles of Christ. Read it," I tell him, "and there's nothing you can't find a verse to fit."

"It's my first night out," he says. " And nobody's gonna blow it. Especially not some fucking Bible salesman." Shaking his cue stick. "A year and a day. A year and a day I was in. And tonight, first night back, you show."

"Your turn" - the other guy, talking to me but looking at the kid - "Next round" - stumbles around the table, spilling beer.

"Ladies' night," the kid says, and the guy, getting his balance, echoes, "Ladies' night."

"I beat up a cop," the kid says. "Nine hundred dollars damage, what the judge told me. Six months from taking it as a minor. Six months, I get a year and a day." He gives me his profile in the light. "I look my age, don't I?" He likes the pose, drains his beer. "Carded me when I come in. Shit, I grew up here."

"You ain't growed up nowhere," the guy says. "Go on and shoot."

The kid fakes throwing his bottle. The

guy ducks, jerks himself over to the bar. "Okay, okay," the guy says. "My turn."

Rita comes out in fresh eyeliner, lipstick, loop earrings. The kid's saying how in prison he got plenty dope, a killer stereo, stayed fucked up all day listening to music.

"Show me the scar," he says.

She's like, "I showed you." But now he's telling me: "I had a girlfriend. First week I was a trustee, I did her in the courthouse parking lot ... but once I got to Raiford, man, no way ... still, she stuck by me. Came every three days, the whole year."

"And a day," the guy says.

"There to pick me up, minute I was out. And what did I do?"

"What you had to," the guy says.

"I blew her off," the kid says. "Soon as I got home."

Rita says. "Kiss me."

But it's me, up close, pinching the dark blue gash of her scar.

"I seen a guy in for raping a five year old," the kid says. "Been stabbed so many times he had scars all over him, like a pin cushion."

The other guy's over the kid's shoulder: "Come on," he says. "Let's play."

Rita drops her hair and walks to the bar, even barefoot like she's in heels.

"I want a real drink," she says.

Nobody's listening.
The guy asks the kid: "Tonight?"
Backing out, I believe him.

Lena

First night on the Outer Banks - Graveyard of the Atlantic - I'm sure of one thing: not to rush it. I work the pier - meet a chick where it sways when a good swell rolls through. I'm drinking local water with ice and sugar to kill the taste, kicked back on the dry part of a bench watching two men shark fishing. She comes around from behind and takes my cup - almost spits it up - "You ought to have a real drink out here, night like this."

I follow her to the bar at the base of the pier. The joint's thick. The band's jamming. I lose her first thing ... find her later dancing by herself in the corner of the bathroom, out of her mind. One of her friends comes up. "What'd you do to her? What'd you give her?"

"I'm getting me a four-wheel drive," she says. "A pickup. A Ford pickup." She goes through the motions of shifting gears. "Get down some dirt roads." And through the beer the accent's getting thick, pure Gates County: "So far back in the pines the sheriff don't know. Do some mudding. Serious partying. Me and my truck."

Works for the phone company, off to spend time with her pregnant sister, dating this guy can't keep a job.

"I spend my life," she says, "making

other people happy."

She's not complaining, she likes it, so that's how it is, I tell her, revenge, how the point is to punish, even yourself. Only she doesn't listen. She just keeps talking about the boyfriend and the pregnant sister, how it "affects her," until her friends show up and decide to take the car, an old slant six Dodge with push button - belongs, the friend tells me, to the girl tripping, wrestling to get behind the wheel.

"It's my car," she says, "I'm driving." But she quits grabbing for the keys when she discovers the radio.

"Drive," I tell her friend.

"I can't," she says. "I never have."

I feel like going back to the end of the pier, seed the water with pig guts and blood and set deep leaders for shark, but instead I get in, get it started. They're both talking, the radio's too loud, the engine's knocking. So I wind it up in neutral, punch low. The rear end torques like the axle snapped, and when it bites I slam in second, run it up till the oil light flashes, the transmission's about to let go, then ease into high down the main two-lane, and the girls go quiet fast, the vibration about to break out the windows, and all I get for one savage mile is the sound of the tires, the wind whistling in the vent, the slant six over-revving. The girl tripping starts going off about her boyfriend again, the lead guitar in the band at the pier, who walked out, she says, first set, and how she can't find him, looked everywhere, and how necessary he is, for her, and for the band, and how these bands in Tidewater, she says, "can't replace him, they need him, he's too good" - suddenly frantic, grabs the wheel, yells, "You gotta find him, you got to."

Her friend pops her and she slumps off, but jerks the wheel so we nearly clip a mailbox. Pops her again and she lets go.

Her friend says, "Headlights."

I brake to the speed limit, the oil light goes off, the temp comes down, but you can smell oil burning off the block ... I turn the radio to a soft whine behind the wind. Switch on the lights.

"Least now we're legal," she says. And the girl tripping sits close to the window, holding on to the dash. "Up here," she says. "Pull over. I need cigarettes."

I hit an all-night chain store. She hands me a twenty, says, "Kools."

I get out and start walking back along the highway, the sky deep black like the water beyond the pier. "Hey," she says. "Hey. The twenty."

I don't need the twenty. I need a reason.

She says something but I lose it in the

sound of the waves beyond the dunes. Cut back across the lot anyway, go inside. The kid behind the register is nervous. Nineteen, twenty. I come in fast, at the counter before he's ready. Seems more uptight when all I want is cigarettes. Then he tells me he can't cash the twenty.

I ask him, can't or won't.

"Not just for cigarettes," he says.

I consider the kid's nineteen years. The price of the cigarettes. The girls out in the car. Ask him, you ever hear of a slant six? He backs away. "It's an engine," I tell him. But he keeps backing toward the deli counter, picks up the phone, goes, "Don't come any closer."

"So dependable," I tell him. "Detroit had to quit making it."

He says, not with a twenty, and stays by the phone. I start thumbing a rack of postcards, but the girl blows the horn, so I grab a throwaway camera, the cigarettes. She doesn't even ask for the change, just opens the pack and lights up, waves the fire in front of her face.

"What're you doing anyway?" she says. "With us, here, now?"

"Visiting," I tell her.

She says I don't look like I'm visiting.

"Purpose," she says. I look like I have a purpose.

Yeah, I tell her. History. Research. Tell her, I'm here to finish a trend.

"Pirates?" she says. "You studying pirates?"

"Flight," I tell her, and pull out the camera. "The Wright Brothers Memorial." I get a few shots in before she starts slapping me. I keep snapping. The other girl's unfazed. I pocket the camera, get in and drive: search some backwoods development for the guitar boyfriend.

"I know when people are pulling things over on me," the girl says. She's got another cigarette going, and just watches it float in front of her face. "The problem is I've got too many friends ... too many guy friends."

We're prowling now, the girl going window to window.

"It can't stop there," she says. "I want to be friends, and they want to be more."

I'm riding the brake on the Dodge, checking every driveway for the guy's pickup. "You can't miss it," she says. "It's white and blue with pink trim, chrome mags, tinted windows."

"Awesome," says her friend.

"And we're getting married," the girl says. "See?" She holds out her hand to show me some ring. Ashes fall in her lap. "He loves my baby, too," she says.

Her friend takes the cigarette, pulls a deep hit and gives it back.

"She's not living with Mama forever." She throws the cigarette out but it hits the doorjamb in a shower of sparks. They both panic, brushing fire off their legs. Only I'm still looking, circling every cul-de-sac, each new subdivision. The girl with money says we should've got beer.

When I pull over this time I get out with the car still rolling, manage to swing the door shut and step clear while the Dodge veers left. I cut across the yard two lots over, to the house I recognize, crouch by a spigot in a bunch of azaleas, turn the water on, just let it run until all I can hear is the pump and the ocean a half-mile away. The stars are fading, but the moon's light enough through the pines, so I can make out the contours across the street, where I'd been before, same transitional time of the year, same dead end of winter - only this time there's no snow, no isolating cold to relax into.

Last time she tells her husband: "What would you do?" And he goes: "What we've got?" Upstairs I drank his brandy, grooved by his fireplace, and when she came in the room she had her hair pulled back like it was a social visit. I walked over to her sitting in her dress and boots, grabbed her face and finished my drink. Her husband was hammering something in the basement, and she could've stopped any part of it, from when I shoved her off the couch until she finished it by the basement door, only she never made a sound, not even when I might've hurt her: just pulled her dress up, buried her face in the pillows, like it was going on without her, so she could tell herself later she wasn't there ... after she poured another brandy, she sat on the couch like nothing happened - her husband still hammering away downstairs - started in about his project, his job, their summer plans.

Not this time.

I cut the spigot off but keep coughing until I get all the water out, get everything out, feel empty enough to kneel by the low side window of her living room and tap the glass. The room's empty but immaculate, like she's hired some company to clean it, like it's some occasion, like she's expecting a guest - still, the same couch, same fireplace, same dining room table her mother gave her.

I try the side door but it's locked, dead bolt, and the window too, over the kitchen sink, shut with some safety latch I can't force without breaking the glass. It'll be light in an hour, but I've come too far, so I lay out the bundle: a pocketsize red-letter healing edition Bible, a Phillips head, a rusty paring knife.

She told me, last time, she had a new

life.

"You believe everybody," she says. "Why not me?

Because of the way, I tell her, she undresses every move.

But now I stick the bundle back in my jacket, edge around the house to the bedroom window, find the air-con unit. The screen's a cinch. They're in a four-post bed with a canopy. But before I squeeze through, some shape in the dark stops me. At the foot of the bed. A cradle. A wooden cradle. The project. The trophy.

I drop outside. Spread the bundle, finger each item. Then I hear the Dodge, see the erratic headlights in the pines, leave the bundle open on the side door welcome mat and run for it.

The last shot I get is of the Wright Brothers Memorial, where the sea goes silver in the early sun, the savannas fan west to the pine flats, and you can see, from the top of the dunes, how what they took from the sea ended up in flight...

Joe

Joe and Rita sit in chairs on the patio. The only light comes from inside. Joe's wearing pleated khakis and loafers with no socks, Rita jeans and a tight white T-shirt. She's holding a washcloth to her face, and when I come up she goes inside. He's cleaning some buds in a tin ashtray using the edge of a pack of papers to sift the seeds from the dope, twists the bone with one thin sheet, perfect as a cigarette. Lights it. I take a hit and start to pass it back, but he motions for me to keep it, cleans and rolls another.

"You're soaked."

The skin between my legs is raw from walking. The salt stings, and the dope makes everything worse at first, but I know it'll work. I hit it hard.

What would you do?

Drive. Anywhere.

I don't know if it's been ten minutes or ten seconds, or if I'm supposed to say something, but now he says, "Everybody thinks I sold Eddie's debt."

It's not a question, so I let it go and keep huffing the joint.

"I know you've heard."

I keep smoking, don't say anything.

"I sold a debt once," he said. "The brother of a chick I was balling. I never carried through, just arranged it, in case. Called the guy on the phone, asked if he was gonna pay. I told him I gave him two months and he'd bought a car and a stereo and all this other crap. Told him a guy would collect, he could pay him instead."

I think he's finished. "What happened to Rita?" I ask, but he's not through. He says: "I'm talking about my girlfriend's brother, man. He paid the next day. Her mother comes up to me, her mother, says, 'you think you're pretty hot, don't you?' Hell, I was fucking her and her daughter too. I just laughed in her face."

He keeps telling it but I'm stoned and thinking how ice won't help Rita's face. Plus the morning's coming fast, the sun about to break, and I know Joe's wired into his second day because it looks like his eyes are bleeding. He rolls another joint and I hang onto it when it comes to me. Rita calls him from the kitchen.

"I'm getting sick of her," he says. I offer a hit but he waves it off, goes inside. The radio comes up loud. Then he's sitting across from me again.

"You worried?"

I shake my head, see behind him the first hint of morning. I light a roach, smoke it alone. The radio dies when the sun breaks the top of the clouds.

"Why would I fuck with a guy like Eddie?" Joe says. "He's more of a zero than Rita."

"Forget it," I tell him.

"You act like nothing happened," he says.

"What happened?" I say. He doesn't finish. Or maybe I don't hear him finish. I say I'll see you. But I haven't left. I'm sitting there and he's still telling it. I hear the radio again. Recognize a song and stay with it.

"Take it easy," Joe says, but I wonder what I would've done: Joe in the bathroom, the gun on the sink, Eddie believing in this fuck he had nothing to do with.

Then we're inside with the curtains drawn. It's dark but I can see the bruise on Rita's face. I remember Joe walking off toward the beach. Rita's wearing a pair of Joe's underwear and a white T-shirt. She's sitting back on the couch, brushing her hair.

"You're afraid of him," she says, sits up and drops her brush on the table, looking better in the dark, the lines in her face much softer. She strikes a match that lights up her cheek, her neck and hair, and I feel it again: slumping off.

"Do me a favor," she says, rubbing ashes into the carpet with her toes. "Get some cream for me."

I go in the bathroom for the jar of

stuff she wants. A cricket's in the sink. I turn on the water and watch it struggle before I lift it out and flick it away. I rub some cream across my forehead, glance in the mirror. Think: this is the dream you don't wake out of. Think: she's nothing I don't make her. Then I hear different music, that Rita and Joe brought back from Jamaica. When I go out, I hope she's dancing, but it's Joe I run into. I watch myself in the silver cap of the jar. Rita comes in from the music, her tough body outlined beneath her T-shirt as she crosses through a crack of light between the drapes, Joe's underwear riding her hips, the dark bruise sunk in her face.

Of course Joe doesn't say anything until he sets his marble cutting block on the table in the middle of us and chops out four lines, each about eight inches long, rolls up a twenty and does two, one in each side, sits back, drops the bill and pinches his nose, says, "Little girl comes down the beach alone out of a cottage holding this baby doll, only it's just the head and body, no arms or legs. This yellow patch of nylon sticking out for hair." He bends down, does half a rail in one side, finishes it in the other. Rita takes the bill from him.

"The kid's wearing this bright orange bikini bottom, no top. Two little bee stings for tits."

Halfway through a rail Rita laughs and scatters the rest of the pile. Joe snatches the bill, scrapes together the lines again and hands me the bill. I tell him no thanks. He looks at me like I said something wrong, then he turns back to Rita and hands her the bill. "Try again," he says, squeezing his eyes as if it hurt to laugh.

Then to me: "She's splashing around in the water, knows I'm watching her. Dries off the doll, wraps it in her towel, starts talking to it, combing out the nylon..."

Rita looks away like she's trying to see something else in the room. "I'm changing the music," she says.

"Leave it."

"I'm changing it."

When she stands, Joe snatches her down.

"Let it play."

And right then the music stops.

"Okay," he says. "Change it." And he lets her go.

She walks to the kitchen sink, tilts her head back and snorts water off her fingers.

Joe lights a cigarette, slaps the inside of his arm. "I know a guy kicked heroin three times. Weeds, no way."

Eddie holds out his hand. I reach for the nail.

Joe chops out another batch. A different song plays. He watches the door to the room but Rita doesn't come through. He rolls the twenty again and does a fresh pair, sits back and runs his finger over his gums.

"Lotta sugar."

He rakes out two more lines. Rita walks back in, and when she sits down this time he hands her the bill - "That drip's the sugar." - relights his cigarette. Rita bends over the coke and bangs a line, pinching her nose and tossing the bill at Joe. She looks at me. "You feel like playing or you scared of him?" Then she snatches the bill back and blasts another finger-thick rail.

"He ain't Eddie," Joe says, Rita carefully puts the bill down on the marble.

"That little girl on the beach finally walked over to where I was standing," Joe says. "I wanted to take off but I swear I couldn't move. She comes up squinting at me and holds out her hand. 'For you,' she says."

Joe squeezes his eyes it's so funny.

"Hands me a goddamn ghost crab."

Rita has the blade, makes a few rough chops, opens her wrist and tries to do the other when Joe comes out of his chair. She hangs onto the razor, chopping at her arm until he kicks her hard and she drops it. I can't move. I watch him give her a sharp pop in the jaw, push her through the hall, hear the bump when he drops her in the bathroom.

I put down the cream.

"We've got to help her," I say, but don't mean to, don't want to go in there, make it to the hall before I hear Joe cock the gun. The hammer clicks, chest high. Then Joe spins the cylinder, points at his face. Joe looks cleaner than ever, and the flash blanks everything. I break for the bathroom, kneel in the dark. Rita grabs me.